What I Heard in the Hall

by Gracine McFie

illustrated by Anna McFie

Published by Wealth Solutions, LLC
7848 West Sahara Ave
Las Vegas, NV 89117, U.S.A.
1-866-502-2777

Printed in the United States of America
Edition: First
Printing: First

ISBN: 978-0-9967612-2-2

"To my future children, nieces and nephews."

My children sat down in a circle on the ground,
And begged for a story as the evening came around.

With a candle on the shelf,
Casting light 'round my chair,
I smiled quite happily as my eyes met theirs.

My story begins way back when I was small,
And my parents took me aside in the hall.

They said to me, 'Son, we have something to say,
About living your life, day after day:

Our first piece of advice is be friendly and nice,
Always say what you mean, and mean what you say,
And never forget to put things away.

Laugh and have fun, relax in the sun,
Enjoy time with friends, make sure everyone wins,

Look after your health, believe in yourself,
And remember, dear Son, that this equals wealth.

When choosing your friends keep this message in mind,
Some folks on the *outside* appear to be kind.

But...

...look at their life and the story it tells,
Some people's life feels like living in hell.

And you don't want that, why that would be bad,
So don't just pick anybody there is to be had.

Remember that you are an amazing creation,
Not something that happened with no preparation.

You mean ever so much to God up above,
Who will guide and protect you with His great love.

Just trust Him completely, and go where He leads
And you will be blessed beyond all belief.

In life you will find that some people work,
Others pretend to, but really they shirk.

A worker who's working is winning his game,
Regardless of title, rank, status or name.

And the choices you make and the work that you do,
Will greatly assist you to win your game too.

Some people give of themselves and their time...

...Some people pinch, save and hoard every dime.

Now giving is good, but a word we must say,
About how to give, in the right kind of way.

Some people give just for others to see,
Like only at church or in front of TV.

Other folks give cause they really do care,
They love to help others and that's why they share.

We're all faced with choices of many a kind,
But the most important of all choices we find,
Is the choice that decides what goes into our mind.

Our mind is amazing, and people have found
That our mind likes to think about things it's around.

So choosing the right kind of music to play,
Or a movie to watch or the right words to say,
Will greatly effect your mind every day.

The things that you eat are important as well,
Like carrots, tomatoes, potatoes and kale.
Strawberries, apples, ice cream and cake,
Salad, spaghetti, chicken and steak.

Your body gets energy from eating these foods.
When you think, work and play this energy is used.

There are also some not so good things you could eat,
Like candy and soda and juice that's too sweet.

Your body then works as hard as it will,
To try to make use of this not so good meal.

But you will be fine 'cause you eat good stuff,
And know how to stop once you've eaten enough.

And now let us talk for a bit about money.
Money's unique in the way it is made,
Money is used as a fair way to trade.

Before we had bills that said One, Five and Ten
Folks used other things to trade with back then.

Like flowers from the meadow, or the bark from a tree,
Feathers from birds, or shells from the sea
A bone from a fish, or a stick, or a stone,
Or a bright shiny jewel from a fancy king's throne.

It could be a rock, or a nickel, or dime,
Some people think of their money as time!

But here is a note that is truer than true,
Make sure you tell your money what it should do,
You never want your money to take charge of you.

For the moment it does, oh the moment it does,
That time in your life will be the worst that there was.

But you'll be quite safe cause you'll use money right,
And so you'll be able to sleep well at night.

Dear Son, that is all that we wanted to say,
And now take this money and put it away,
And carry it around in your pocket each day.

46

You don't need to spend it, you don't need to lend it,
Or fold it, or tear it, or hide it, or bend it,
Just keep it safe with you wherever you go,
This will make you feel comfortable with money you know.

And someday when more money comes into your hands,
You'll use it with ease like a responsible man.
And both of us know that your money will grow,
Cause both of us know that your money will flow.

And you will succeed because you are smart,
And that is the message to you from our hearts.

54

"And so, my dear children, the words that I speak,
And the story I told you, is yours now to keep.

"Live, laugh and learn, rejoice and have fun
Your game is awaiting, it's time that you won!"

About the Author

Gracine McFie is a natural born story teller. Since early childhood she has entertained her siblings, both older and younger, with tales about nature, make believe and humor. An avid enthusiast of classic children's literature, she can quote entire passages by heart from Dr. Seuss, Aesop's Fables, Mother Goose, Grimms Fairy Tales and many others.

Gracine's brilliant ability and talent serves her audience well. She also enjoys flying, playing the piano, crocheting, sewing, drawing and spending time with her toy poodle.

About the Illustrator

Anna McFie is a gifted artist. Besides her talented use of the pen in writing and drawing, she is clever with a paintbrush, crochet hook and guitar pick. As a purpose driven young woman you'll never find her lying about, but rather using the talents of mind and hands to create, serve and entertain.

Anna enjoys, learning new things, sports and spending time outdoors